D0505111

Little Funnies is a delightful collection of picture books made to put a giggle into storytime.

There are funny stories about a laughing lobster, a daring mouse, a teeny tiny woman, and lots more colourful characters!

Perfect for sharing, these rib-tickling tales will have your little ones coming back for more!

TEE HEE!

HA HA!

To Ellen, for all her help
P.R.

To my grandson Will,
with love
H.C.

SOGGY SATURDAY

Written by
Phyllis Root
Illustrated by
Helen Craig

WALKER BOOKS
AND SUBSIDIARIES
LONDON · BOSTON · SYDNEY · AUCKLAND

One Saturday on Bonnie Bumble's farm, it rained so hard it washed the blue right out of the sky.

It rained blue on the chickens.
It rained blue on the cow.

It rained blue on the sheep and the pig and the grass and the trees.

When the rain stopped,
everything was soggy and blue.
Blue eggs.

Blue milk.

Blue wool.

"This can't go on," said Bonnie Bumble, feeling blue herself.

So Bonnie got busy with brushes and buckets. She painted the chickens all speckled and brown.

She painted the cow all spotted and yellow.

She painted the sheep
all creamy and white.

She painted the pig
all shiny and pink.

She painted the grass and the trees all green. She even got out a ladder and painted the sky all cloudy and blue again.

Soon everything was the right colour on Bonnie Bumble's farm. "I'm glad that's over with," she said. And it was ...

except for her little dog, Spot,
who had splashed in all
the buckets.

First published 2001 by Walker Books Ltd
87 Vauxhall Walk, London SE11 5HJ

This edition published 2007

10 9 8 7 6 5 4 3 2 1

Text © 2001 Phyllis Root
Illustrations © 2001 Helen Craig

The moral rights of the author/illustrator
have been asserted.

This book has been typeset in
Calligraphic Antique.

Printed in China

British Library Cataloguing in Publication Data:
a catalogue record for this book is available
from the British Library.

ISBN 978-1-4063-0787-0

www.walkerbooks.co.uk